El Pájaro de la Luz

Maya Fernandez

Para mi Abuela

Somewhere, hidden in a quiet village lived a wise, old woman and her two curious grandchildren engulfed by the wildness and wonder of the ancient jungle. On the night of the full moon, Mama sat by a fire alongside Apu and his older sister Pacha.

Mama told them stories of magic and danger, warning the siblings to never venture beyond the village. "The jungle is home to creatures that tower over the tallest man, floors that pull you into the Earth and a darkness that goes on for days," said the old woman. "Those who leave, never return."

Pacha fell asleep with her grandmother's tales weighing on her mind, frightened by the outside world. The same could not be said about young Apu, who waited for the perfect time to escape and explore the jungle.

Pacha was awoken by the sounds of rustling outside their hut, only to discover Apu had found his way into the jungle in complete darkness. Noticing her brother's fresh footprints on the dirt, Pacha gathered all her strengths to follow them into the jungle and return with Apu before sunrise.

As the young girl made her way into the wild, she noticed the glaring faces from behind the trees and strange sounds that rang through the dark. Pacha looked worriedly at the river current that stretched through the length of the jungle. Suddenly, a large glowing figure emerged from the water and turned its face to look toward her, boasting "I am the Cayman of Colors, and this river is my home. What is your purpose here?" Pacha, frozen in bewilderment, told the cayman of Apu and her mission to bring him home. He replied that her brother had arrived at his bank earlier, and would allow her to cross the river as he did Apu. The cayman then stretched his immense body over the river, as Pacha tiptoed along the scales of his back. Before she could give thanks to the colorful creature, the cayman had already crept into the water and disappeared.

Feeling confident about her last encounter, Pacha walked along the forest with more ease than before. "If the Cayman saw Apu not long ago, then he must be close," she thought to herself. Hopeful as she was, the night had gotten darker and the canopy above her rustled with the movement of the animals that lived inside. While Pacha squinted at the forest floor in hopes of finding more prints, a spotted snake the size of five men lifted her off her feet and tightened its grasp on her body. "Help me!" screamed Pacha, as the warning her grandmother gave her rang through her head.

Just when Pacha began to lose hope that she could escape from the spotted snake, she felt herself released from its grip, suddenly flying through the air. As the snake slithered into the trees, Pacha was pulled into the high vines by a jumping monkey with bright red cheeks. "This jungle is no place for a young girl to be wandering in, especially at night," said the monkey as he sat her on a branch. " I have come in search of my brother, but it is too dark to find my way to him. If only there were a way to see his footsteps again," said Pacha. The monkey told Pacha of a magical bird whose light has the power to illuminate the whole forest.

Pacha and the jumping monkey looked for miles along the jungle floor in search of the Bird of Light. She was found perched under a large tree atop a dirt hill. The young girl looked in amazement at the long, colorful feathers which reached the lengths of the tallest plants around her. Pacha, determined to return home to her grandmother with Apu, made her way up the hill and told the Bird of Light of her journey to find her brother, and her reason for finding her. The Bird of Light replied, "You are brave to travel through this jungle on your own. This light will lead you and your brother home before sunrise safely."

In seconds, her feathers flickered with patterns and colors more vivid and beautiful than anything Pacha had ever seen. The eery darkness of the jungle began to vanish in the brilliance of the Bird of Light. Suddenly, Pacha could see her brother's steps on the floor again, and they looked to have lead just over the hill. Pacha expressed her gratitude in a number of thanks, to which the Bird of Light nodded and pointed her head toward Apu's footprints.

Pacha ran down the hill, embracing her brother in relief and joy to have found him. Hand in hand, the siblings walked through the illuminated forest and the stories and perils that the both of them had along the way. While returning to the safety of their village, Apu and Pacha looked back on the adventure, beauty and magic that lives in the jungle, and felt happy in calling it home as well.